Insubordinate

Charles deAnne

First trade paperback edition 2024

Cover design by Alexandria Dallman

Edited and typeset by Nick May

ISBN: 979-8-218-45225-4 (paperback)

This story is based on actual flying experiences of the author. While these experiences were real, and their settings and circumstances are historical facts, they only serve as context for the fictional story woven from the imagination of the author.

External dialog (in quotes), internal dialog (in italics), and first person narratives are fictional. Any conjectures, inferences, and opinions are founded, not on facts, but rather on a vacuum of facts. All of the flights described in this book share one thing in common: Total absence of after-action acknowledgement or feedback. After each incident, everyone acted as if it never happened.

Without validation, the mind fills that void, and constructs a hypothetical reality to provide rational continuity between past and future—a mental bridge between what we know happened in the past, and how to evaluate what's happening now.

To Jim, Bill, Pete, and Matthew. In memory of Marci.

Contents

Escape Vietnam ... 3
Welcome to NAS Corpus Christi ... 11
A Miracle for Dee's Twenty-Third Birthday ... 15
The Accident ... 25
The Instrument Check ... 31
What Goes Around ... 45
Mystery Submarine ... 53
Lessons from Pelicans ... 61
Sequel ... 73
Death of the Proud Bird ... 87
Trouble with Harry ... 99
Dee's Nightmare ... 103
On Thin Ice ... 105
Future Causality ... 109
First Pre-flight of a Boeing 707 ... 115
Machu Picchu ... 121

1

Escape Vietnam

March 6, 1966, US Naval Air Station, Sangley Point, Philippines.

The Continental 707, MAC flight, is on the NAS Sangley Point tarmac, ready to go. I'm the last passenger to board, having waited to make sure all of crew three made this flight home—the 'Big Island.' We almost missed it. I persuaded the Continental captain to wait twenty minutes for a few stragglers.

Our new squadron C.O. (acting) appears not amused. *Queue up, Commander, I've got bigger sharks circling my boat.* It occurs to me that Commander C.O. Stark, C.O., might have been destined to be a commanding officer. His parents might have recognized the strategic advantage of names, like *Major Major Major* in *Catch 22*.

Stepping over the gap between the air stairs and the forward entry door, I show my ticket to the flight attendant—4A. I make a right turn and crawl over Lieutenant Quinn in the aisle seat, wrestling my carry-on duffle bag into the space under 3A.

The overhead compartments are already latched. Probably packed like *Fibber McGee's* closet.

Clicking my seatbelt, I find a place for my feet. I push my duffle left and put my right foot on the floor beside it. Raising my left foot, I use the back of 3A's armrest as a footrest.

A ramp agent, after sticking his head in the cockpit and giving some papers to the flight engineer, leaves through the forward entry door. He pulls a handle on the door, which is folded forward toward the nose of the airplane. The entry door swings from its open position outside the airplane to its closed position inside the cabin. *Neat trick, the door swung through an opening smaller than the door.*

Through my left window, the air stairs are moving away from the airplane. A flight attendant rotates a long aluminum lever, counterclockwise, then unsnaps a red ribbon and resnaps it across a small round window in the entry door. The engines are starting as several flight attendants station themselves at intervals along the length of the 707.

The front flight attendant narrates her well-rehearsed demonstration of donning the May-west, inflating it by pulling on the tab or blowing in the tube. She continues, "Oxygen masks will drop automatically if the airplane loses pressurization. Pull sharply on the mask to start the flow of oxygen. Don't worry if the bag does not inflate. Oxygen is flowing..." My mind can't help racing through everything she's *not* saying.

How hard will I need to yank on that flimsy little plastic tube to start the oxygen? How much oxygen is flowing if the bag isn't inflating? If the bag doesn't inflate, why is it there? I decide that if I'm ever on an airplane that depressurizes at 41,000 ft., I hope I'm in the cockpit with those big-ass O-two tubes, attached to quick-donning masks. *Would an airline hire a pilot who has only landed on water in the last four years? Forget it, Hoff—I promised Dee I'd get an engineering job.*

As we taxi, Lt. Quinn has his left leg crossed over his right knee. I notice the contrast between his shined black shoes and my scuffed cordovan toes. I've always preferred the casual aviation green uniform over the more formal blues. *Would I have been promoted to full lieutenant if I'd paid more attention to shoe-shine skills than flying skills? Probably not!*

####

I finally feel my body start to relax. If the admiral were going to stop me, he would have done it before they buttoned up the aircraft. Still, I feel relief to hear the gear doors close shortly after rotation. The 707 rolls out of a left bank and is climbing at a steep body angle—I estimate 20 degrees nose up.

The sun is straight out my side window, low over the South China Sea. Corregidor Island, in the mouth of Manila Bay, is still clearly visible, but moving rapidly aft toward the left swept wing, with its two Pratt turbine engines protruding forward from its leading edge. *It's real—we're outta here!*

Lieutenant Quinn is the squadron's intelligence officer. We haven't spoken since boarding. *He might have been expecting a call from the admiralty!* My suspicion is confirmed by his first question, "How the hell did you get out of the P.I. without getting court-martialed?"

My go-to defense is play-dumb—"What are you talking about?"

"You know damn well, Hoff! Anyone else in the squadron, including the C.O., would have been court-martialed for lying on the O-club floor and saluting an admiral from the horizontal."

"That was the straightest brace and sharpest salute he'd ever seen, Quinn! Besides, I'm the lowest-ranking PPC in the Navy—below an admiral's dignity to punch that low—and it would expose his deficient sense of humor."

"What about this morning? We were all expecting a CAT-5 shit storm when we heard your fake *off-report* for your replacement aircraft, while it was still here in Sangley. You had direct orders to not take off from Cam Ranh Bay until your replacement aircraft sent an *off-report.*"

Quinn doesn't need to know what the admiral and I know. I was told we had to wait for the off-report because we were included in the daily operational status report. Three-Boat had been cannibalized—we were not operational. The admiral was either lying on his status report, or he was lying to me. I don't think the admiral wants to explain either case in a court-martial.

"You said you heard an off-report! We heard it too—luckily, it was just in time to make it back to Sangley to catch this flight."

Quinn shakes his head incredulously, "Hoff, I understand why you're still a *jaygee,* but I can't figure out how you became a patrol plane commander and got your own crew."

"You're ahead of me—I don't understand either one."

Actually, I have a pretty good idea why I was passed over for Lieutenant, but I have no clue why the squadron still promoted me to PPC. Maybe our C.O., at the time, received an original copy of my training folder. It couldn't have been the official version, authorized by the commanding officer of advanced training—the first admiral I crossed swords with!

I've always liked Dick Quinn, in spite of our polar opposite attitudes toward the Navy. I know I've been a pain in his ass—created a lot of extra paperwork for him, as the squadron's intel officer.

When Three-Boat had the ready-alert, and the Air Force lost a Russian trawler it had been tracking, I stayed at 2,000 feet, running in on each radar contact on a widening circle around its last position. When we identified the trawler, I descended to 200 feet and made a close pass off its starboard side.

A few days later, Quinn called me into his office to inform me the United States had received its "four-thousand-and-something" serious warning from the Soviet Union. "How close were you from the trawler when you made your pass?" he asked.

"About a thousand feet," I said, as he pushed an 8 X 10 glossy toward me. "Great camera! Can I get a copy? Three-Boat's shark teeth really look good." I remember seeing Quinn's signature head shake.

Luckily, the trawler crew was too slow—they didn't get a shot of our bomb-bay doors open. I had used them as speed brakes to dive quickly enough for a single pass.

Tired of Quinn's inquisition, "I've had a day, Dick. I'm going to check my eyelids for leaks."

Pushing my thumb on the concave button on my armrest, my seat back moves a couple inches aft. I pull down the slide shade on my window, closing the scene of the setting sun, the South China Sea, and the horrors soon to come with the rapidly approaching darkness beyond the western horizon.

My eyes are closed, but my mind is far from sleep. I've completely changed in just four years. I don't recognize the person I was in spring of '62—fresh from basic flight training with top grades in the T-28—gung-ho—couldn't imagine insulting an admiral in the Officer's Club.

I must have brain damage from the car accident—the Navy knows! How was I able to complete flight training—even stay in the Navy?

Adjusting my head to face the plastic window shade, I signal time-out from conversation. My past starts playing like an inflight movie I have no control over.

2

Welcome to NAS Corpus Christi

When did my Navy career go south? I think it started with the first order waiting for me when I checked into Advanced Naval Aviation Flight Training, NAS Corpus Christi, Texas. I was ordered to report to the commanding officer of the entire advanced flight training program.

I couldn't imagine that every new student was required to meet personally with the admiral. *He might want to congratulate me on my grades in basic flight training—especially the instrument training in the Link trainer.* Those WWII vintage, generation-zero flight simulators were designed to eat a new student-pilot's lunch.

In my senior year, someone donated an old beat-up Link trainer to East Waterloo High School. After duct-taping over leaks in its four accordion bellows, it flew pretty good—if you didn't know any better—the air pump was weak, making control response slow. Not as bad as the three-inch play in my '37 Chevy's steering wheel, though. I had hundreds of hours teaching myself how to fly instruments before I'd touched a real airplane. *Never felt a need to disclose that experience to the Navy.*

I knocked and heard a gruff "Come in!" from the other side of the door. "Ensign Hoff, Sir."

The admiral didn't look up from the folder on his desk. He didn't offer me a seat, so I remained at attention.

Finally, "Looks like you have pretty good grades in formation and gunnery, Son."

Pretty good? I had actually hit the target! Pretty good was what you got for not putting holes in the tow plane. I decided against correcting the admiral on this point. "Thank you, Sir."

"So, let me get this straight, you have an aeronautical engineering degree." (I could hear him thinking, *Paid for by the US Navy.*) "You have the flight grades to fly anything in the fleet, and you're requesting the P5?"

"Yes, Sir!"

He looked at me for the first time. "You afraid to fly jets, Son?"

"No Sir, I just want to fly seaplanes." If I had told him I wanted to get stationed with my friend, Mike Nickell, I knew he would make sure we got stationed on opposite sides of the globe.

"You're dismissed!" He scribbled something on the paper in front of him. The context of his dismissal was unmistakable: *Get out of my sight, you coward.*

I did an about face and left the admiral's office. *That went well! What the hell was that all about? Did he call me in just to insult me? If the Navy wanted to assign the airplane they wanted me to fly, they could have done that! Why did they give me the choice—like he said—to fly anything in the fleet?*

Walking to my VW bug, I can't wrap my head around the admiral's visceral anger. I thought the Navy was still interested in anti-submarine warfare. The Martin 'Marlin' P5M seaplane was designed for ASW! Sounds like he thinks ASW is a waste of talent.

That was my welcome to Advanced Naval Aviation Training and the end of my Navy career.

At least I knew what to expect—the best possible reward for a job well done will be no punishment.

####

My thoughts return to the unbelievable reality of the Boeing 707—*I am actually going home! I will be out of the Navy in a few short weeks, and with luck, have "Honorable Discharge" stamped on my DD-214.*

I readjust my position to change pressure points. I keep my eyes closed in case Quinn is still awake. *Don't invite another inquisition.* I let my brain continue its silent inflight movie—it skips over unrecorded long periods of amnesia. I have only a few memories of advanced training that I know are my own—the others are things that Dee has told me so many times I know they're true, but come from a different place in my brain—like remembering a book or story that I wasn't really a part of.

3

A Miracle for Dee's Twenty-Third Birthday

My flight with Jock, in the Stoof, is my next memory I know is mine—it's etched in my neural network—an indelible recording, hardwired in read-only memory.

The Grumman S2F "Tracker" was our first introduction to multi engine and multi pilot flying. This phase was to prepare us for our multi engine instrument check, which would be flown from the left seat; therefore, students were not trained in the right seat.

After a few weeks of training, I was paired with another student, *Jock*, for our "solo" flight. We each were to make three landings as pilot-in-command in the left seat, with the other student acting as copilot in the right seat.

The S2F had a short fuselage, to fit as many Stoofs as possible on an aircraft carrier. The wings fold up, hinged just outboard of each engine—the same radial engine that was on the Navy's T-28. The engines were really close to the fuselage to minimize engine-out yaw torque—so close that the prop tips almost touched the fuselage just behind the pilots' heads. With cockpit side windows that bulged out, you could lean outboard and look straight down, but if you looked aft it was a little spooky—you were looking right into the prop disk just a few inches from your head.

Even with its engines as close as possible to the fuselage, the short rudder-to-CG moment arm required a three-section compound rudder to balance engine-out yaw torque with one engine at full power, and the other engine shut down. Bottom line—the S2F was a beast to control with an engine out. Without immediate pilot action, the S2's short tail results in an extreme yaw toward a suddenly failed engine, potentially leading to the dreaded 'stall-spin-crash-burn-die' sequence.

Jock was a NAVCAD (Naval Aviation Cadet). NAVCADs were student pilots who were not yet officers—they got commissioned when they got their wings. Since I was already an officer, I flew first (I pulled rank) with Jock in the right seat flying copilot. My flight must have been uneventful—I don't remember anything about it.

That changed after we set the parking brake and switched seats—I remember every second of Jock's flight. Terror, I think, increases synaptic discharge voltage to the point where neural pathways cauterize into permanent connections.

After Jock's first takeoff, as pilot-in-command, I had just raised the gear and was calling Navy Corpus Tower for a clearance downwind for a touch-and-go. I felt the aircraft swerve with a sudden yaw to port. Looking up, with my mic still keyed, I noticed Jock had only pulled #1 throttle back to climb power.

The S2F's two throttle handles are attached to two thin side-by-side levers, hanging down from the overhead between the two pilots. Together, the two throttles form an upside-down 'T.' From the left seat, the pilot needs to hook both throttle handles with his right hand, by straddling the two levers with his fingers. The pinky and its neighbor on the #2 (right) throttle handle, the index finger and the naughty one on the #1 (left) throttle handle.

Jock had all his right fingers on #1 throttle! There were no warning lights or any indication of an engine problem. I reached up with my left hand

and touched the back of Jock's right hand to show him he only had ahold of #1 throttle. As soon as I touched him, he slapped my hand away, jerked #1 to idle, and punched the #1 feather button!

I still had my mic keyed and changed my request: "Uh, Navy Corpus, requesting a full stop with an engine out." Navy Corpus announced on guard channel that the field was closed. They cleared us for an immediate left downwind.

Apparently Jock's sum knowledge of flying twin-engine airplanes consisted of three simple rules:

1. "Step on the ball to center it." (The black ball is in the curved glass tube, called a slip/skid indicator.)

2. "Working foot, working engine." With #2 at takeoff power, and #1 pulled back to climb, Jock was pushing hard on the right rudder to keep the ball in the center. He must have concluded that since his right foot was working, the left engine had quit,

3. "Never turn into a dead engine." (I'd like to find the guy who told him that.)

Having followed rules one and two, Jock was now stuck on rule three. I couldn't get him to make a left turn for the approach. He was frozen on the controls—wings level, 300 ft, full right rudder, ball centered, #1 punched out, and #2 at full power.

"Come on, Jock, we're cleared for a left downwind. Ball's in the center—we're in balanced flight—we need to climb to pattern altitude and start a left turn."

No response! Jock was frozen at the controls. His right leg was shaking—he hadn't trimmed a lick. We were still at 300 feet, 300 knots and passing over Padre Island. With nothing but the Gulf of Mexico ahead, I was starting to worry about the 5-minute limit on full power. If we blew #2, there was no place to go but down.

Tower was yelling at me. I was yelling at Jock. Jock was totally locked up.

I tried another tack, "Jock, why don't you give me the airplane so I can get it trimmed up for you." (As if I had some crazy intention of ever giving control back to him.)

Jock put his hands in the air, “Okay, you’ve got it.”

I announced, “I’ve got the aircraft!” Jock was off the yoke, but he was still pushing on the right rudder. I gradually fed in right rudder trim so Jock would see the ball go left of center and realize he was pressing too hard on the right rudder. It appeared he was totally focused on keeping the ball in the center. Finally, when he was no longer pushing on the right rudder, and the ball was centered without rudder force, Jock put his foot on the floor.

I pulled #2 back to climb power—backed off on the right rudder trim until the ball was centered, without rudder pressure. I started a climbing left turn, back toward Texas.

Abeam midfield NAS Corpus, on a normal left downwind, I started the flaps out and put the gear handle down. Abeam the touchdown zone, with three green gear lights, I called, “One-eighty, three in the green.” Corpus tower cleared us to land.

As I banked left to start a standard Navy circling approach, Jock said his first words since giving me control. "Where's the airport?"

"Right out your side window!"

Jock turned his head left and announced, "I don't like the looks of it—I want to take it around."

"NO, WE'RE LANDING!"

Jock went crazy. He got back on the controls and started fighting me. I could over-power him on the ailerons, but he had regained his leg strength. With the right rudder trim (I had put in) helping him, he was able to put a leg-lock on the right rudder.

I was holding a steep left bank, and adjusting pitch to stay on the approach arc. With Jock standing on the top rudder, the aircraft was in an extreme side-slip throughout the approach. I was glad I hadn't yet reduced more power on #2, or selected any more flaps than I had on the downwind.

The approach was so ugly (FUBAR is the correct term), the landing safety officer turned his back on us when we were at the 'ninety'—he didn't want to see the inevitable crash.

We came across the runway threshold at 50 feet, 30 degrees left bank, with the aircraft nose pointed 30 degrees right from the runway direction.

I'm not at all sure what happened in the next second—whether I stomped on the left rudder to break Jock's leg-lock or Jock gave up and took his foot off the right rudder or divine intervention—or all three.

The airplane rolled wings level, the nose swung left, and we stalled onto the runway centerline. As soon as we hit the runway, I pulled #2 to idle and shut it down.

I called for a tow off the runway. Jock and I were put in separate rooms to write our narratives of our versions of the flight. While we were writing our reports, they unfeathered #1 and ran up the engine—nothing was wrong with it. If we had crashed, no one would have known who's fault it was.

Jock was washed out of flight training, and I was quietly put back on the flight schedule. I often wondered if the admiral heard about that incident. *Of course he did! He must have read my report! I shut down his flagship, NAS Corpus!*

Never heard, "Nice job."

Never heard, "Thanks for saving the airplane."

I did, however, get the Navy's best reward for a job well done.

It was June 6, 1962—Dee's twenty-third birthday. I went home and announced, "Happy Birthday, I brought you me." (That quote was provided by Dee.)

I have total amnesia from writing my narrative until three days later.

4

The Accident

It's dark. My mouth is full of blood. I probe inside my mouth with my tongue. The broken end of my left jaw bone is where my front lower teeth should be. I go back to sleep.

I woke up to questions from an EMT. He must have told me I had been in a car crash. I remember my questions, but not his.

"Is my wife all right?—Is our baby okay?"

I remember hearing, "There was no woman or baby in the car, sir."

My next memory (of my own) was sitting in a hospital, waiting my turn for an operating room. Dee was with me. We saw a man in a wheelchair—a cage around his head—wires, dozens of wires, each attached to part of his face or head, with their other ends stretched radially outward to the cage.

We were told he was the driver and only person in the other car, and Mike and I were the only people in Mike's car. I asked where Mike was. Dee told me that he was in an operating room. It must have been hard for her to lie to me—they told her to tell me that—they said I couldn't handle the truth right now.

Of course! It was a Naval hospital! The Navy's first instinct is to treat everyone like mushrooms. *Keep them in the dark and feed them shit!*

My next memory is in the hospital with a roommate, a NAVCAD, who had both legs in traction. My jaw had been put back together, held in place with wires up and down across the gap left by my missing lower teeth. I could only eat through a straw, but I was lucky compared to my roommate. Aside from a few teeth, I had only lost some skin and flesh along my right arm and hip from skidding on concrete.

Dee visited me every day—almost all the time I was awake. I don't remember how long it was before she told me Mike had died at the scene. He was DOA at the hospital.

I don't know which was stronger—my anger, or my guilt. Why did I live? Why did Mike die? Who or what has the power to manipulate physics—who guides the thousands of high-velocity lethal parts and decides who dies, and who lives, in the microseconds it takes to convert the kinetic energy of two vehicles into twisted metal, static heat, broken bones, and pools of blood?

I think it was the guilt that was the worst—probably because I could hide it. My anger couldn't be contained.

I soon recognized my personality had changed and realized I needed to control my rage if I was to have any chance of returning to a normal life.

My oral surgeon, a Navy captain, prescribed a whole egg blended into my oatmeal for more protein in my diet. Some sailor, just following orders, threw a 'whole egg,' shell included, in the blender!

Instead of seeing the humor in the mistake, I hoisted myself out of bed, got in a wheelchair, rolled into the captain's office, slammed the oatmeal on his desk, and said, "You eat this shit!" (In retrospect, it might not have been *just* the admiral who killed my chance of promotion in the Navy—the captain might have had a role.)

I started hearing a male voice in my head. He said his name was Bob. It was weird—he seemed so real—had to be coming from my own brain—some kind of delusional anomaly.

Bob started talking to me often in the hospital. He gave me reassurance and advice, "You're going to keep flying, Hoff, but you need to get control of your temper!"

I took Bob's advice. I learned quickly.

####

The flight with Jock was June 6, 1962. My logbook records another solo flight on the eighth, then my first instrument training flight on the ninth. I have no memory of either flight. Dee has told me that Mike came over to our house in the afternoon of the ninth and we went out to the base to go swimming—we didn't get there.

I had obviously told Mike the details of my flight with Jock. My last memory of Mike was him saying, "I've never been in a situation where I thought I was going to die."

If I hadn't had those two flights on the eighth and ninth, I probably never would have flown an airplane again. I knew that I had pulled off a miracle in the S2F, with Jock fighting me on the controls. Still, without the push from Dee, I wouldn't have continued flight training.

Two months after the accident, my wire braces had been replaced with rubber bands. The doctor cleared me to fly with a pair of nippers hanging around my neck, in case I got air sick.

Partly because I was driving her crazy, partly because she realized the Navy would not *invite* me to resume flight training—she kicked me out of the house. "Put your uniform on and hang out in the ready-room—drive *them* nuts—read the manual and bug them until they put you back on the flight schedule."

It worked! My logbook shows my first flight after the car accident was on August 16, 1962. On my next three flights, I logged 23 landings. I was back! I owned the S2F! Even more than the T-28, I knew I could handle anything they threw at me!

5

The Instrument Check

My inflight movie involuntarily fast-forwards to October 3, 1962:

I was expecting a workout on my instrument check. I had imagined the debates that must have occurred behind the scenes. Why did they even let me continue training? They must have assumed I wouldn't be able to pass the instrument check after all that had happened. The Navy knew I received a major concussion in the accident. This would be a way to wash me out, and make it my fault.

The check ride, however, was beyond anything I could have imagined.

I had never met the check pilot before. That's normal and intentional—*no bias going into a check ride.* I don't remember a preflight briefing, but that doesn't mean there wasn't one—my brain's video recorder started with pulling the instrument hood over my head and snapping it in place on the glare shield.

We started out with basic warm-up maneuvers—intercepting and tracking radials, holding entries—easy stuff. Then a weather problem forced a diversion to College Station for a VOR approach to runway 10.

I can still hear the VOR identifier: "dah-di-dah-dit, di-dah-di-dit, di-dah-di-dit," then a male voice, "College Station VEE-OOH-AAR," the East Texas accent drawn out and emphasized. (We were expected to read rapid Morse code, but to understand voice, we needed to hear it real slooow.)

I had to listen to the identifier for the entire approach. As soon as I tuned the VOR, things turned to worms. I never had time to turn the volume down.

Right after I intercepted the 100-degree radial inbound to College Station VORTAC, the check pilot simulated an engine failure by pulling one engine to idle. I ran through the engine shut-down drill, without cutting the mixture or feathering the prop.

I know the check pilot is not a suicidal maniac like Jock—besides, the prop is still turning. *Nothing scary here!*

I trimmed pitch for approach speed, and trimmed rudder for ball centered with power set for level flight.

I reviewed my secret for hand-flying an instrument approach. *I'm flying that old beat-up Link trainer in high school! Sloppy controls, slow response, unforgiving of untrimmed elevator force—muscles can't keep a constant force without feedback—if I'm holding any control force, I can't take my eyes off the attitude gyro for a split-second—pitch would change—airspeed would change—altitude would change—vertical speed would change! I need to test the pitch trim every few seconds—put an air gap between my hand and the stick—make sure the airplane stays where I want it—hands off!*

Keep it simple, Hoff—trim for a constant airspeed—only descend with wings level—only turn with altitude level. Only one thing moving at a time! Juggling an actual IFR approach is hard enough, without extra balls in the air.

I had just a few seconds to glance at the approach plate before station passage. I scanned for the essentials: *280 degrees outbound (Good, I'm already on it!), 100 degrees inbound (Of course—the reciprocal), standard procedure turn on the south side of the approach course. Don't need the outbound or inbound procedure turn courses—a forty-five degree left turn to outbound, then a one-eighty right turn to inbound.*

Burn in the altitudes! 2,000 feet procedure turn, 1,300 feet at the VOR inbound, 880 feet minimum after the VOR—make it 900—easier to remember and will give me a twenty-foot pad for an overshoot. Of course, knowing what I know now, I would never let myself get rushed into an approach—especially with an engine out, or, on a check ride. I should have asked for a holding pattern to get squared away.

Station passage! Hack the clock! Start down to 2,000 feet! I pulled the power back. *Don't trim the rudder—keep the ball in the center with rudder—should be back in trim when power is set for level flight. Unlike the elevator, I can lock rudder displacement with my heel on the floor.*

Just as the VOR needle on the RMI started to settle down from its wild swings directly over the station, an 'OFF' flag appeared at the top of the RMI. *No problem! He failed the radio-magnetic-indicator when I was already on a two-eighty heading—my compass will be frozen like this throughout the approach—this is exactly what it will look like inbound from the procedure turn—both the tail of the VOR needle and two-eighty heading at twelve o'clock, even though I'll be going the opposite direction.*

Piece of cake! I'll just pretend the tail of the needle is the head of the needle when I'm inbound. Right now I just need to stay on the two-eighty heading and level off at 2,000 feet. Descending through 2,500!—add power, keep wings level, keep ball in the center by releasing rudder pressure as power comes up. I leveled off at exactly 2,000 feet with the tail of the VOR needle still at twelve o'clock. *Perfect!*

Oh, shit! Did I hack the clock over the VOR? Doesn't matter—don't know the elapsed-time from station passage to procedure turn. How long did it take to descend to 2,000 feet after the VOR and level-off? It must be at least a couple minutes. I told the check pilot, on interphone, "Call procedure turn outbound."

As the check pilot called approach control, I rolled into a left standard rate turn. I checked the second hand on the clock. *OK, I need a forty-five degree left turn. Primary compass frozen—whisky compass not accurate in a turn—'dip angle' and all. I need to hold a standard rate turn for fifteen-seconds—a ninety degree turn on the second hand, since it turns twice as fast as the airplane in a standard rate turn. Time's up!*

I started to roll wings level. Another 'OFF' flag—this time on the attitude gyro. *Great! I'll have to fly the rest of the approach with the attitude gyro frozen in a thirty degree left bank. Wish I could just cover it up. I can do this! Needle, ball, and airspeed! Wings are level if the turn-needle is straight up and ball is centered—keep airspeed constant—power controls vertical speed.*

The attitude gyro was hard to ignore, but I continued to roll right, until the turn needle was straight up, indicating the aircraft was holding heading. I was still level at 2,000 feet and checked pitch and rudder trim.

Just as I was feeling confident that I was holding constant heading and altitude on the outbound procedure turn leg, I realized I hadn't checked the clock when I rolled wings level! I needed to guess at the time again. I felt sweat dripping out of my flight helmet.

Adrenalin was screwing with my perception of time. It seemed like an hour since I started the approach. *I need to keep the aircraft within ten miles of the VORTAC. Now another 'OFF' flag—the DME! I can replace distance-measuring-equipment with time—another minute should do it.*

Thirty seconds later, I can't make myself wait any longer. I checked the position of the clock's second hand and rolled into a right standard rate turn. *OK, I've got to hold this for a full minute! A three-sixty for the second hand is one-eighty for the airplane.*

Holding the turn, one needle-width right of center, ball centered, altitude steady at 2,000 feet, I could sneak a peek at the clock every few seconds. *Second hand coming up on its starting position. Time to roll out for the inbound procedure turn leg.*

I rolled out of the right turn, trying to ignore the attitude gyro, still showing a thirty degree left bank. When the turn needle was straight up and stabilized, I glanced at the compass. Since it was frozen at exactly 180 degrees from the inbound approach course, the tail of the VOR needle should be straight up when I was on the approach course.

Oh shit! It's already there! I need another right forty-five now! I rolled back into the right standard turn and tried to hold it for 15 seconds. I might have overshot the time, but then, I wasn't too sure about how standard my standard rate turn was.

Just as I got straight and level figured out again, the VOR needle started swinging wildly. Station passage already? I must have shortened the entire procedure turn and intercepted the approach course just outside the VOR.

They call it the *cone of confusion*, where the airplane is directly over the VOR and its precise direction from the VOR is ambiguous, and the VOR needle swings randomly. *On this day, on this approach, 'cone of confusion' is a gross understatement.*

Shit! I'm still at two thousand feet. I'm supposed to cross the VOR at thirteen hundred! I'm seven hundred feet high!

I brought the working engine to idle and kept the ball in the center with rudder. I ignored the compass. Coming out the east side of the VOR with the compass frozen and upside down from where it should be, and the VOR needle pointing backwards, I was totally confused. Would those two opposite errors cancel? Should I turn toward the head of the VOR needle, or away from it? I decided not to look.

The best I could do was to keep the aircraft going straight and hope I was on a 100 degree heading. With the attitude gyro frozen in a 30 degree left bank, and the compass frozen upside-down from where it should have been, I had to focus only on the instruments I could trust: needle, ball, airspeed, and altitude.

OK, Hoff, keep the ball centered, turn needle straight up, and don't bust minimums! Approaching nine hundred feet, I brought the power up and let up on the rudder pressure to keep the ball centered.

OK, now what? I'm at minimums. I don't know what the missed approach DME is. Doesn't matter, DME is out, and I don't know the missed approach procedure anyway. I'm lost!

I was about to key my mic and confess that I had no idea where I was. The check pilot keyed his mic, "I've got the aircraft! Pop your hood."

This is going to be ugly! I popped my hood, expecting to see nothing but trees. Instead, there was a runway centerline straight ahead. The check pilot requested a touch and go, threw the gear out, and selected landing flaps. After touching down, he zeroed out the rudder trim, spooled up both engines, reset flaps, and took off.

He did it all, all the way back to Corpus. He never asked me to tune a radio or get a clearance. My flight suit was soaked with sweat. He never talked to me—not one word. It was weird. No debrief when we got back. I didn't know I passed the check ride until I saw my name on the flight schedule the next day.

When I realized that the check pilot was not going to debrief me, I had a fleeting urge to ask him if we could schedule another flight tomorrow? We could change seats and he could demonstrate the proper way to fly that approach with an engine out, compass frozen upside-down, attitude gyro frozen in a 30 degree bank, and no DME.

Then I remembered Bob's advice: "Expressing your anger might feel good at the time, but it's counterproductive. Don't go out of your way to make enemies."

As we walked across the tarmac from the S2F I thought: *He didn't have to tell me to pop my hood at the missed approach. He could have waited a few minutes until I had overflown the runway, and then told me I blew it. Instead, he demonstrated I had put the aircraft in a perfect landing position. This check pilot might be my only friend in the Navy right now.*

I have rerun that check ride hundreds of times, and know I never could have done it again, even at my peak proficiency. I believe Mike was sitting on my shoulder.

####

I woke to the sun, low over the Pacific, coming in through the windows across the aisle. I looked at my watch—only midnight. Quinn was awake. "Short night!" he said.

"Going to be a short day, too. We're only half way through our fifteen hour flight." I can see the flight attendants loading a cart in the galley. "I need to visit the blue-room to make room for a cup of coffee." Quinn unbuckles and moves into the aisle.

He repeats the maneuver when I return. As we get situated in our seats, the carts come out in the aisle. "Welcome to yesterday, again," I quipped.

"How's that?"

"Sunday in San Diego, Monday in Manilla!"

"Oh, yea. It always gives me a headache, just thinking about it."

"It doesn't get easier. My body still crosses the dateline just fine, but my brain has to go around through Greenwich. It takes about a week for my brain to catch up with my body."

####

Throughout our short second *yesterday*, Quinn avoided questioning me. When the captain announced the start of our descent, the view out my side window was identical to the one I had had on departure—different ocean, a third of the way around the Earth, and our second sunset for the same day.

The seat belt sign comes on. I'm thinking about Dee. I say, "Hope they let the wives come on the North Island ramp."

"Must be nice having someone waiting for you. I guess I'm married to the Navy."

"I can't wait to see Dee!" Quinn and I are on different planets.

"What's your wife like?" Quinn asks.

I'm taken aback by his unexpected and unwelcome question. Has Quinn forgotten the long tradition of topics off-limits between officers and gentlemen? Politics, religion, and women!

I paused, then, "Well, she's a redhead, left handed, and pretty sure she descends from a long line of Celtic warriors. She's like the slick pages of a Sears catalog—doesn't take any shit off anyone!"

6

What Goes Around

Late March, 1966: Destroyer, U.S.S. ????

My last temporary duty assignment before my discharge on May 1, 1966, was to conduct an operational readiness inspection for a destroyer while it sailed from Monterey to San Diego. A copy of my orders for this TDY is not in my service record, but my best guess is that it was during the last two weeks of March 1966.

Most of VP-48 went to the Galapagos on a boondoggle—a well-deserved R&R, having just returned after *nine* months of a *six*-month deployment. I understood why I was not invited. The purpose was to boost morale. Why waste the squadron's Bravo funds on a J.G. who's getting out of the Navy in a few weeks.

The only thing that will boost my morale is seeing North Island's two huge Quonset-hut-shaped blimp hangars in my VW bug's rear-view mirror. But, conducting an ORI for a destroyer? Doesn't seem to fit my resume.

I can't remember the name of the ship or the name of the captain, but I do remember introducing myself when I arrived on board, and I remember him letting me know I was the lowest life form he had ever had aboard his ship. He told me to do whatever I needed to do, without getting in the way of anyone on his ship, especially him!

I understood why he felt that way. After all, I was just a lieutenant junior grade, *and* a pilot. Maybe he was jealous of the extra ninety dollars, hazardous duty pay. Still, I was taken aback by his loud public announcement of his personal feelings.

I felt I was being baited. Maybe someone tipped him off that I have had a problem showing deference and respect for rank. It might have been the admiral I had saluted from a horizontal brace in the Sangley O-club. *Just because I'm paranoid, doesn't mean he's not still out to get me.*

I also remember looking at the ship's organization chart before conducting the required man-overboard drill and noticing a dashed line from the chaplain to the captain. Only two people report directly to the captain, the XO and the chaplain.

After the welcome aboard speech I received, I imagined what the chaplain's might have sounded like. *"...do what you need to do on Sundays. Just don't get in the way! And when we're at sea, there's only one God on this ship—me!"*

For the man-overboard drill, I hid the chaplain.

On the bridge, I announced, "Man overboard," to the captain. He ordered, "General quarters!"

After the first muster, everyone on the bridge knew who was missing, except the captain. With everyone *present and accounted for*, the captain said, "I don't think you hid anyone."

"Yes, Sir, I did."

"OK, we'll do another muster."

After the second muster, everyone on the ship knew who was missing, except the captain. "You did *not* hide anyone!"

"Yes, Sir, I did."

The captain's neck veins were bulging. "OK, we're doing one more muster, and if you're messing with me, your ass is grass!"

After the third muster, everyone in the Pacific Fleet knew who was missing, except the captain.

The captain and I repeated our now familiar exchange:

"You did not hide anyone!"

"Yes, Sir, I did."

"Who?"

"The chaplain, Sir."

The captain addressed everyone on the bridge, "Who does the chaplain report to?"

I answered for everyone on the bridge. "That would be you, Sir."

I've always been curious how the captain's Navy career went after my ORI report. Probably just fine, but I'll never know. The chances of my report being in the official Naval archives are about as likely as the MAYDAY I would send the next month.

I do not have an issue with rank. My issue is with incompetence, arrogance, and hubris, combined with absolute power over life and death.

The destroyer would be docking in San Diego at 0900 the next morning. I knew I wouldn't see the captain again. That night, in my stateroom, I couldn't sleep, even though a rocking ship usually knocks me out. I tried to remember exactly when my cognitive dissonance started.

That fissure between my core beliefs and my duty as a Navy pilot, I think, started during the Tonkin Gulf crisis. I was a copilot when VP-48 was tasked with keeping a P5 on station, 24-7.

My logbook shows my first sortie from Sangley was on August eighth. The day after the House of Representatives passed the Tonkin Gulf Resolution.—Wait, that was the same day! The Seventh, in Washington! Might have even been before the resolution passed—definitely before it was signed by President Johnson, on the tenth. The Navy was spring-loaded!

Bob might have been right after all. He always said the pretext for that resolution was based on a lie. He called us "tethered goats." He comes up with some crazy shit, though, never sure when he's messing with me.

Bob had stopped talking to me after I got out of the hospital. I started using him though—blamed him for anything I misplaced—started calling him my invisible time traveling monkey. I started hearing Bob again when I was patrolling the Tonkin Gulf, flying around our assigned holding pattern in the most dangerous airspace on the planet.

On my back, in my bunk, enjoying the pitching destroyer, its bow crashing rhythmically into the long slow swells of the Pacific, and thinking about the sting I had just pulled off. *It could have backfired. I was lucky, no one on the bridge slipped the captain a note with "chaplain" written on it. He must be a real asshole to everyone.*

Then I heard Bob."Just to set the record straight, Hoff, you come up with plenty of crazy shit all on your own. And by the way, Hoff, even when you go deaf to me, I can still hear you."

"Doesn't seem like a fair arrangement, Bob. Anyway, I'm not in the mood for invisible monkey fun tonight. Why don't you go wherever you go when you're not here; I need some sleep."

"It's not where, it's when, remember? By the way, you've just humiliated this captain, Hoff, and if it was a setup, you've got a lot of enemies in high places."

"Okay, whenever."

"Just saying, Hoff, paybacks are hell, and you're in a lot of crosshairs!"

"I'll be careful, Bob, might even shine my shoes!"

Bob was gone. Probably thinks I'm too cocky after my big win. He might be right. I trusted his insight in Tonkin Gulf: "The Navy needs to get rid of the P5s anyway—if they shoot one of you down, it's all good—one problem solved, and their righteous indignation justifies escalating this shit-show, or whatever they call it."

After that, I saw only two ways to resolve my internal conflict in Vietnam:

I can suspend my core belief system to allow my duty as a Navy pilot—go all in with the war—see any assigned target as a legitimate combatant, even if it's a running naked girl, covered with burning napalm.

Or, I can carry out any legal order that doesn't conflict with my core beliefs—but define the line I will not cross, even at risk of court martial and prison.

I was lucky. The mission of the P5M in Vietnam was primarily surveillance, and, of course, taunting the enemy with tempting, easy bait.

7

Mystery Submarine

April 6, 1966 NAS North Island, Coronado, CA

Two-Boat, the XO's airplane, was scheduled for a night tactical ASW flight, as part of VP-48's operational readiness inspection. Three-Boat was the backup for Two-Boat. The XO called in sick. I was assigned to replace the XO as patrol plane commander on Two-Boat, flying with crew two, the XO's crew.

There was a target U.S. submarine in the exercise area. Our mission was to find it. After taking off west from San Diego's North Bay sea lane, we arced left, staying halfway between North Island and Point Loma. Clearing the southern tip of Point Loma, I banked right. The radar operator fired up his scope.

First sweep, he reported a target ten miles west of San Diego. Our Tactical Air Control Officer marked it on his scope. Next sweep, it was gone! A sinker! The sub captain must have panicked and pulled down his periscope when we first painted him. If he hadn't pulled his scope, we would have thought it was a small fishing boat.

Why would the target sub be running with its periscope up? Seems too easy for an ORI. Okay with me—It'll be a short night!

TACO gave me a vector to the target. As the vector approached twelve o'clock on the RMI, I rolled wings level and descended to 50 feet on the radio altimeter, to maximize the chance of the sub triggering magnetic anomaly detection. First pass, TACO called "MAD contact!" on interphone.

I pickled off a flare. Flares launch out a retro-tube that is set to the aircraft's ground speed. They come out the back of the aircraft with zero ground speed, like the *Roadrunner*, and fall straight down.

I kept the wings level for 15 seconds while climbing to 200 feet, then a left steep turn, holding 45 degrees bank for 270 degrees of turn, which put the flare at 12 o'clock. With wings level, I descended again to 50 ft and flew directly over the flare. "MAD contact!" I pickled off the second flare.

I went on the gauges and repeated the above maneuver. There were now two flares in the water. Steep turns had to be flown strictly on instruments. It was a clear night, with stars above, and flares below, all looking the same. I couldn't risk confusing one for the other. *Trying to fly over a star is as bad as trying to fly under a flare.*

Only after completing the 270-degree steep turn and rolling wings level could I safely go visual.

TACO vectored me to the last flare dropped. Descending to 50 feet again, I aimed for a point where the sub should be if it hadn't changed course or speed. "MAD contact!" I pickled off the third flare.

We now had three consecutive MAD contacts. The sub was in an escape-proof MAD trap. The first MAD contact was pure luck. The sub must have been really slow or on a course that was closely aligned with our initial run-in.

The second MAD contact was mostly luck also, but it provided a good course and speed during the two minutes it took for the first lobe of our cloverleaf pattern. The third MAD contact was pretty much a sure thing. It would also catch any change in course by crossing the sub's course at 90 degrees.

The next MAD contact was a done deal. On this fourth inbound run, I would be flying along the course between the last two flares but correcting for any turn indicated by the course between the first two flares. The crew prepared our attack signal, consisting of five practice depth charges. (Each PDC contained the equivalent of 25 pounds of TNT.)

"MAD contact!" I pickled off another flare, plus five PDCs. I thought this was going to be the fastest sub-hunt in history. I expected the submarine to immediately surface and grade our attack. Nothing! No radio call.

I went back on the gauges and started another steep turn, still expecting a radio call before I could complete another lobe of the cloverleaf. Nothing! No radio call. "MAD contact!" Pickled off another flare, plus five more PDC's.

We continued the cloverleaf pattern for three hours, getting a MAD contact on each pass and dropping another flare, along with five PDCs.

When we ran out of PDCs, I broke off the attack, climbed to 1,500 feet, and made VHF contact with our practice sub. It was seventy nautical miles north.

I couldn't sleep that night. What was I tracking? Had to be a sub—a lot of iron to make that magnetic anomaly. It was moving—no radar echo—it was a sub! Why didn't it surface? We were bouncing those PDCs off its hull! If it was ours, wouldn't the captain surface and call us on 'guard'—tell us to "knock that shit off"? One hundred twenty-five pounds of TNT, every two minutes! Was it Russian?

I heard Bob! "I could tell you, Hoff, but I'd have to kill you!"

"Where have you been?"

"When, Hoff, not where! Didn't think you needed me for a while. That was a nice touch, hiding the chaplain—no captain will ever fall for that one again! Anyway, I've been doing some research."

"So, what's really going on here, Bob?"

"Sorry, can't tell you, without changing history. For a time-traveler, that's fatal—it would change temporal continuity—equivalent to hitting a mountain with your airplane. Well, Hoff, I can tell you what you need to do—make the things happen that need to happen."

"I'll bite! What's that, Bob?"

"In a few days, the eleventh, there will be a squadron party at the North Island O-club ..."

I interrupted, "Let me guess, you want me to salute another admiral from the horizontal, again? You can put that on your list of things that won't happen again!"

"You've got me all wrong, Hoff. Just watch your six! This isn't over until it's over! You will be assigned your last patrol in the P5M on the eleventh. Make sure Dee goes to that party! Trust me—you'll thank me later!"

"That's going to be a hard sell, Bob. She won't go alone."

No response! Bob was gone!

The next morning I was expecting a debrief. I was disappointed. We hadn't found the sub we were supposed to find, but it *was* a sub. That was the most perfect MAD trap, ever. Three hours, without missing a MAD contact on every pass!

No debrief? The Navy's best reward for a job well done...

According to my logbook, I flew another tactical ASW mission that night, on the seventh—like my MAD trap never happened. We must have found the right sub that night. I don't remember anything about the flight—nothing weird to remember.

The next day, Lieutenant Quinn pulled me aside and told me the sub I MAD-trapped on the sixth was a Golf class Russian nuclear missile submarine. "This is way beyond both our security clearances," he said, "but I thought you should know."

"Thanks," I said, but red flags were popping up faster than on my instrument check! If it's beyond Quinn's security clearance, why would they tell him? Why would Quinn, an intelligence officer, tell me something above my SECRET clearance?

It took me a few minutes to get it. He wouldn't! It's a lie—oldest entrapment trick in the book.

Feed your target a false, juicy story—if you hear it echoed back, you've got him! A twist on Sun Tzu's rule: "If you hear the same story from two spies, kill them both!" I wouldn't touch Quinn's story with a ten-foot pole.

A Russian sub captain wouldn't be that stupid! Hanging out that close to Point Loma at periscope depth? It was too easy! That charade must have been a setup—a decoy U.S. sub, to get our attention right off the bat. Probably expected me to follow standard protocol—the sub would be back in its berth, on the other side of the Point, before we got our shit together. I'd blow the ORI—no evidence of any sub.

It sounds crazy, but it's the only thing that makes sense! The sub captain wasn't expecting me to run in and start MAD-trapping, without any preliminaries. Now Washington has recordings of the sub, and our MAD-trap track! I think there's going to be some "splain'n to do, Lucy!"

Two days later, on the tenth, the day before the squadron party, I looked at the flight schedule: Three-Boat was assigned the longest patrol we flew out of San Diego—I felt the hairs on the back of my neck stiffen.

8

Lessons from Pelicans

April 11, 1966, NAS North Island, San Diego, California

The VP-48 squadron party at the O-club that evening was the last one Dee would be able to attend. I was scheduled to fly the longest track of any of our patrols out of San Diego—the southern track, reaching south of Isle Guadalupe, Mexico. I insisted that Dee get a babysitter and go to the party. She resisted, but finally agreed, if it was that important to me.

From her account, it was weird. No one talked to her. In fact, she had the impression she was being avoided. She felt like Typhoid Mary. So, she went over to the bar, ordered a coke, and talked to the bartender.

After a while, another pilot's wife came up to her and asked, "Aren't you scared?"

"Scared about what?"

"Don't you know?"

"Don't I know what?"

Then she told her—I had lost an engine at the furthest point of our track. Then she repeated, "So, aren't you scared?"

Dee's long, wavy, auburn hair had another reason to be red—it was on fire! "No, I'm not scared! I know exactly what he's going to do!"

"You do?"

"Yes, he's going to throw everything out of the airplane but the crew, then he'll drop down to ground-effect, and I'm going home to wait for him." Then she added, before storming out of the O-club, "Besides, it's a boat!"

What Dee didn't know was that it's a very small boat, in a very large ocean, and no search-and-rescue aircraft had been launched.

Earlier that morning, we discovered Three-Boat was out of service for a maintenance issue and had been replaced by a P5 we had never flown (Tail #141254). We were told it was ready to go. All our preflight checks looked good, and with crew three aboard, we pushed backward, down the North

Island seaplane ramp, north of the two oversized, Quonset hut-shaped, ex-blimp hangars.

I always flew with a single-engine range chart on my kneeboard. We had just turned north for our home-bound leg when number one suddenly quit. I caged #1 with the feather button and discharged the fire bottle. I checked our fuel remaining. With my finger, I traced from our distance to San Diego, up to the curved line on my kneeboard. We were in big trouble!

We sent a "MAYDAY" on HF—no answer. We transmitted in the blind that we would be reeling in our HF trailing wire antenna and have only line-of-sight, VHF communications available.

I did what Dee predicted. Throwing out everything not welded down was an easy call—dropping the bomb-bay fuel tank, not so much. The tank was dry—we used all the bomb-bay fuel on the outbound leg and we desperately needed to get rid of weight.

I had seen the bomb-bay tank with the bomb-bay doors open on the ground—it was a pretty snug fit. The tank was hung from the bomb release hooks, and I was sure it had been tested on the ground with something rigged to support it, but I had never heard of the tank being dropped while in flight. If it damaged the bomb-bay door mechanism, or worse, got stuck partway, we would be ditching for sure.

Would it be better to wait, so if we were forced to ditch, our chances of rescue would be better? Or, should we do it right away, and if we were forced to ditch, at least we would have plenty of fuel for the APU, and we might be able to rig the trailing wire antenna from the tail to a wingtip or something.

I looked at our fuel flow and realized that sooner was better than later. Every minute we carried extra weight decreased our chances of making it all the way to San Diego without ditching. I opened the bomb-bay doors and pulled the bomb release trigger. No loud, metal-on-metal sounds. I held my breath and closed the bomb-bay doors. It worked as advertised. Thank you, Martin engineers!

With the airplane buttoned up and as light as possible, I trimmed the pitch for maximum lift-to-drag ratio. I asked the crew to take turns sitting in the plexiglass bubble in the tail—originally, a tail gunner's position. It's more efficient to balance the airplane with weight at the tail, instead of aerodynamic download from the horizontal stabilizer. Gravity is free; it comes with the planet; aerodynamic load has a drag penalty.

I kept just enough power on number two for a fifty-foot-per-minute descent. It was going to be a long day for Dick Atkinson and myself, and I was in no hurry to get into ground-effect, where we would be taking turns hand-flying. Only by hand-flying would we be able to feel the exact height above the water, where the nose slightly tucks and the airspeed magically ticks up a few knots. It happens at less than a half wingspan above the surface, for the P5, about fifty feet. (That's the wing—the keel is about ten feet above the Pacific.)

Once you feel it, you know it—it's like surfing the downhill slope of a high-pressure wave created by the downwash of the wing—downwash with no place to go—too low to escape out toward the wingtips, where it would normally form mirror-image, counter-rotating vortices from stolen kinetic energy.

Once established in ground-effect, I checked our fuel flow—still too high. I could reduce fuel flow by leaning the mixture, but operating procedures required setting the fuel flow higher (richer) than the rate of fuel flow that could be completely burned by the available oxygen flow. The unburned fuel was used to cool the cylinders.

If the mixture was set to the chemically correct fuel-air ratio, the cylinder head temperature (CHT) would get so hot, the engine would self-destruct.

I turned to our crew chief, Bolding, and asked if he'd ever leaned a big radial, past the chemically correct mixture, to use excess air to cool the cylinders instead of excess fuel.

He said he hadn't, but would try anything to keep his feet dry. I leaned number two past max CHT, with Bolding monitoring each cylinder. We got the normal CHT drop on all 36 cylinders, and the fuel flow was now going to get us home!

Luckily, just before nightfall, we had enough fuel to climb out of ground-effect and make a normal approach and landing in San Diego's North Bay sea lane. North Island approach control didn't ask if we needed crash boats standing by. *They must not have received our MAYDAY.*

When we were pulled up the North Island seaplane ramp, no one was there to meet us. Not our commanding officer, Commander C. O. Stark, or even the duty officer. *The squadron must not have received our MAYDAY, either.*

It wasn't until I got home that Dee told me. The whole squadron knew we were in trouble, and it appeared to her that no one thought we would make it back. I was anticipating a thorough debrief the next morning.

The next morning the squadron was surreal. No one so much as acknowledged the incident of the previous day. No curiosity! No questions about how we managed to get back when the performance manual indicated it was impossible. I was disappointed.

While Commander Stark might not have had any questions for me, I had several for him. Starting with: Why did everyone in VP-48, and their wives, know we were in trouble except my wife? And why was search-and-rescue not launched when they had, obviously, received our MAYDAY?

I never asked Commander Stark my questions. He hadn't reached out to me, and I read that as a clear indication he wasn't interested. Besides, I was getting out of the Navy in a few weeks and happy to be alive. I just wanted to put a lot of time and distance between me, Vietnam, and VP-48.

I had thought about requesting an inquiry, but even if I got to the bottom of it—even if it brought someone down—I knew the fate of whistleblowers. I would be black-balled from the aerospace industry, or any airline.

I'm lucky! At least, I got the Navy's best reward for a job well done.

If Dee had not gone to the squadron party, I never would have known my last patrol with VP-48's crew three was sabotaged. *"Thanks, Bob!"*

"You're welcome, Hoff! Glad to be of service."

"Glad to hear you again, Bob. What's going on around here?"

“Glad to be heard! I’ve found some interesting coincidences! I can only tell you about things that have already happened, but I can say this much: never trust ‘surprise’ attacks that occur, or don’t occur, on the seventh day of the month!”

“How’s that?”

“Take the Lusitania, it was sunk by a ‘surprise’ attack by the German U-Boat, U-20, on May 7, 1915.”

“Then, Pearl Harbor suffered a ‘surprise’ attack by a large Japanese fleet, while 81 long-range PBY seaplanes were sitting on the ground in Hawaii, on December 7, 1941.”

“Interesting, Bob, but two data points don’t make a convincing correlation. Anyway, how do you correlate things that didn’t occur on the seventh?”

“You might think it’s a stretch, but consider that your first flight to Tonkin Gulf was August 8, 1964, in the South China Sea. But that was August 7, 1964, in Washington, D.C. If a ‘surprise’ attack had shot you down on your first taunt, it would be remembered as the seventh.”

“Catching that mystery sub on April 6: If a ‘surprise’ nuclear attack was planned for the next morning, that would’ve been the seventh! Just saying, Hoff. There’s more, but I can’t tell you. They haven’t happened yet.”

“That is weird! There’s no departure time in my log—just logged as nighttime—might have been the seventh by the time we started the MAD trap. What’s happening, Bob?”

“I don’t understand all I know about it, Hoff. The same pattern seems to be stuck in a recursive loop. There’s a poem about big fleas and little fleas. Might apply to a lot of things—Like,

Old wars breed new wars that feed on their atrocities.

New wars breed future wars,

To the end of all humanity.”

Bob doesn’t talk to me anymore. He still lets me know he’s here, though—moves my glasses from one room to another and, sometimes, from one day to the next.

I don’t always appreciate him as much as I should.

####

A few days later, I checked out of VP-48 and the US Navy. Even though I was officially receiving an honorable discharge, I felt like I was being drummed out. I saw none of my fellow officers that day. My only contacts were with the squadron's enlisted sailors.

I was humiliated and embarrassed, but also proud. Proud of my crew, and their performance on all our missions—and proud of flying the P5M, the last of the Navy's seaplanes. *Thanks, Mike!*

I looked through my copy of my service record. Glaringly absent was the temporary duty assignment on the destroyer, sailing from Monterey to San Diego! I don't think I even exist in the official archives of the Navy. There's probably no record of a pilot, Lieutenant (junior grade) Paul Charles Hoff ever serving in VP-48!

Officially, this story is fiction!

9

Sequel

Monday, November 20, 2023. Boulder, CO.

When I started writing this short story, "Insubordinate," it was my intention to only include the preceding eight chapters. Writing was prescribed therapy, to help me recover from a brain bleed. Symptoms became noticeable in the Atlanta airport when Dee and I were checking in at a United kiosk for a flight to Denver.

At ATL, it took five tries to get my reservation number correctly transcribed from my iPhone. Then, when we got through security, I wanted to get a "Starluck cap of copper." They called it aphasia. I knew what I wanted to say, but the words came out with scrambled syllables.

To make a short story longer, being a guy, having one Y strand of code on my XY chromosome, which includes my invincibility code, without the "death-is-serious" code, which it would have had if it were another X, we pressed on to Denver. That was August 22, 2023.

####

Fast forward to today, 11/20/23: Half awake—early—still dark, I heard Bob! First time since that night after my last patrol, in 1966. My first question, "Where...I mean when have you been? Why did you stop talking to me for all these years?"

"It wasn't me, Hoff. You went deaf to me again. After you left the Navy, I think your brain rewired its damaged areas from your accident. Your recent brain bleed might have put you back on my frequency."

"Like I said, nice hearing you."

"Like I said, Hoff, nice to be heard!"

"I've started writing again. Hope you don't mind. You're part of it."

"Always have been, Hoff, and I think it's time you know the truth about a lot of things—hope it will be therapeutic."

"Sticking around awhile? I've got a pretty long list of questions, but I don't feel ready to get fed with a firehose."

"I don't know, Hoff, depends on how long you stay on my frequency. I think you really need closure on that last patrol, though."

"Did I remember it right? Did I miss something?"

"No, you got it right as far as you went. However, you didn't do a thorough aerodynamic analysis of theoretical 2-dimensional flow. You didn't calculate the effect of eliminating all induced drag—no drag penalty for aerodynamic lift—the best you could expect from ground effect."

"I didn't need to! It got us home."

"Yes, but that was a big mystery for the Navy! They ran through all the drag reductions you should have gained, using all the tricks you used—you should *not* have made it back to San Diego!"

"They never asked me anything about how I did it!"

"They didn't have to. Anyway, they came to the conclusion that you had help from some technology they don't understand. They think it might be an anti-gravity device."

"That's crazy, Bob! I don't have any technology they don't have. Not now, and certainly not in 1966!"

"Well, there's a few coincidences that got their attention!"

"Like what? And who are *they*?"

"Here's the what, Hoff. On April 6, 1966, just hours before you caught the Russian nuclear missile sub off the coast of San Diego, there was a mass UFO sighting near Westall High School, Melbourne, Victoria, Australia."

Bob interrupted me preemptively. "Hoff, there were many reports of UFO sightings that Project Blue Book was eventually forced to release. In one, a missile launch officer at Malmstrom AFB testified that a UFO hovered close by, while all ten of the missiles he controlled went offline. That incident reportedly occurred in 1967, but I believe it actually occurred while you were MAD trapping that Russian sub!"

Bob continued as I tried to process the implications. "The who—I don't know for sure—but at the top of my list would be General Curtis LeMay.

One thing I'm sure of, it was way above the pay grades of the two admirals and the destroyer captain you pissed off."

I interrupted. "Did LeMay, or whoever the spooks were, think there were UFOs helping us catch the Russian sub?"

"Even if they didn't, that's what they wanted the Russians to think. They wouldn't want the Russians to know that a twice-passed-over, insubordinate, smart-ass pilot, about to be kicked out of the Navy, flying an obsolete seaplane, just accidentally stumbled on their nuclear sub as it was preparing to launch the first nuclear strike of WWIII."

"Thanks for the glowing resume, Bob. If you're right about our ICBMs shutting down, they certainly wouldn't want Russia to know about that, but why would they want to kill me and my entire crew?"

"Just telling it how it was, Hoff! What did you expect? A medal? No punishment? Maybe an apology? The Navy's official opinion of you was fixed ten minutes after you walked into the admiral's office in Corpus Christi. The most difficult thing for any person to change is their opinion—for a flag officer who's never had an opinion challenged, it is impossible!"

Bob didn't stop for a breath! Does Bob even breath?

"Yes, Hoff! Embarrassing high command is a dangerous sport!"

I slid some words in sideways. "Why did they try to kill the whole crew?"

"If you were lost at sea, and I think the CIA would have made sure of that, they would have blamed 'pilot error.' After the navy got your sonobuoy tapes and your MAD trap track, they put every ASW resource on that sub's maximum range arc and closed the net. They found it and put a destroyer on top of it—stayed over it until the sub captain either scuttled the sub or the destroyer sank it."

"You're right! They couldn't let the sub get away! But that means the navy knew exactly where it was!"

"*Exactly,* Hoff! The sub you were MAD trapping was K-129. Neither the Russians nor the US would acknowledge that K-129 was missing until two years later, in 1968. The Russians couldn't admit that their nuclear missile submarine had mysteriously disappeared while it was supposed to be launching a nuclear strike against the United States."

"Is the sub still there?"

"You haven't been keeping up with your conspiracy theories, Hoff. The US leaked a rumor that they were able to pinpoint K-129 by using some magic super-secret nonexisting sonar sensing system. The CIA contracted with Howard Hughes to build the Glomar Explorer under the guise of a mining exploration vessel. Its real purpose was to recover K-129. Nothing about K-129 has ever been officially *confirmed or denied.*"

"Is that why you think our spooks thought I was getting help from UFOs?"

"Well, Hoff, the spooks on both sides knew about the UFOs in Australia, and ours knew about our ICBMs getting shut down at the same time you caught the sub. Even if the UFOs had nothing to do with you catching the sub, they knew you were a security risk. You would be out of the navy soon and out of their control, as if you ever were. I think their solution was to sabotage your airplane for that last patrol."

"They must have been shitting bricks when we made it back! They must have known that Dee went to the party and found out the whole squadron knew we were in trouble. They knew I would find out the squadron had received our MAYDAY when I got home."

"Yea, your stock went way up, Hoff, when you brought that P5 back from what they thought was a mission impossible. I think the spooks became more afraid of you than the Russians."

"The spooks took the P5M you flew on your last patrol and put it in an old blimp hangar, similar to the two at North Island. They've been studying it to figure out how you made it back to San Diego."

"I'll put in a FOIA request to find out if it's still there."

"Too late, the hangar burned down a few weeks ago. By the time the fire department got there it was fully enveloped—all they could do was contain it—they let it burn itself out."

"When was that?"

"November 7, 2023! Get some sleep, Hoff. I'll try to talk to you in a few days. Even time-traveling *monkeys* have other things to do than just harass old folks."

"Sorry about that—I made up the invisible monkey story as a joke about my senior moments. I've had my doubts that you were real."

"No worries, Hoff, I like the monkey label—good as any. Every time you hear, 'Bob's your uncle,' it'll remind you, you're not as far from monkeys as you like to think."

####

Bob was gone.

Was that a dream? Was that really Bob? Did he say, 'get some sleep?' Really?

I felt around with my feet and found my slippers. Dee was asleep. I left the bedroom door open so she would see me at the dining table when she got up. I loaded the coffee maker with six cups of water and three scoops of grounds—didn't press the 'Brew now' button. *Wait for Dee, so it doesn't boil down to coffee syrup. Stop making up projects, Hoff. You're stalling.*

I was ambivalent about opening my laptop. Did I want it to be real? Or, did I want it to be a dream? I had to find out. I googled "Hangar fire, Nov 7." There it was—one link was an article from *Stars & Stripes*, "Navy gives $1 million to start historic hangar fire clean-up in Southern California."

It was real! Bob's real! Oh, shit! November 7. This is weirding me out!

Opening my logbook, I thumb to the last patrol: April 11, 1966, serial # 141254, 8.7 hours total flight time, longest flight in my log book for the P5, without using JATO bottles.

That's different! The sailor who kept the logbooks entered "1P" for the flight code. I decoded "1P" in the front of my logbook: 1=Daylight Visual, P=Rescue, Survivor Search (incl. Combat Rescue).

The sailor who maintained our logbooks coded my last patrol as if it was our own search-and-rescue mission! A clever message-in-a-bottle, confirming what I already know—everyone in VP-48 knew my last patrol was sabotaged.

####

I'm still waiting for Bob to come back.

Bob said the Navy didn't need my input. Of course, they interviewed Dick Atkinson and Bolding! They knew how low we were—they knew how we leaned the engine—knew about a crew member in the tail bubble to relieve the aerodynamic download on the tail.

If Bob's right about putting that P5 in an old blimp hangar to study it, they had our exact weight. So what was the big mystery?

Of course! He said they analyzed it as a two-dimensional flow problem—assumed the same lift coefficients required from the Bernoulli equation.

That's it! Bernoulli's dynamic pressure assumes constant density—an incompressible atmosphere—we never consider compressibility until airspeed approaches the speed of sound. A good assumption at altitude, but something very strange happened in ground effect that day.

The nose dropped! We were flying at a lower angle of attack—a lower lift coefficient—requiring more dynamic pressure to carry our weight. The air density under the wing must have increased!

The indicated airspeed increased! Not because the airplane accelerated, but because the increased air density increased the indicated airspeed with the same true airspeed.

We were surfing on the leading edge of a compression wave, created by the downwash of the wing itself! It sounds like perpetual motion—not something a serious scientist would consider, and I'm sure they had some serious scientists working on it.

So, they, LeMay, or whoever, couldn't figure out how we made it back to San Diego, based on what they didn't understand about ground effect!

Quinn was being straight with me! It wasn't a double-bluff! He wanted me to know that I found a Russian submarine, and trusted me to not say anything.

The spooks must have known it was going to happen, couldn't believe I had caught that Russian sub by a fluke! Then, when I got the P5 home from my next and last patrol, in spite of their best effort, they jumped right to UFO technology. Maybe they thought I was an extraterrestrial and had called the mother ship for help.

Just one word to the spooks: Boo!

10

Death of the Proud Bird

I kept my promise to Dee. After leaving the Navy, I got a job with Ryan Aeronautical Company, in San Diego. While enjoying the analytical aspect of flying, both Dee and I recognized I was getting ground sick. Reluctantly, knowing it would mean many lonely nights, Dee agreed to let me apply with an airline.

My starting class date with Continental Airlines was November 14, 1966, a mere six months after my discharge from the Navy.

Almost seventeen years later, after flying one year as second officer (flight engineer) on the Boeing 707, ten years as first officer (copilot) on the Boeing 707, one year as first officer on the Boeing 727, four years as captain on the Boeing 727, and then back to first officer on the Boeing 727, after the hostile takeover of Continental by Frank Lorenzo, I had the most phenomenally improbable flight imaginable: September 24, 1983.

It also turned out to be my last flight as an airline pilot. I was the unscheduled substitute first officer (copilot) on a Boeing 727 Continental flight from Boston, Logan Airport, to Denver, Stapleton Airport.

A week earlier, September 17, my younger sister, Janet, was wed to her husband, Evan, in the quaint little town of Tamworth, New Hampshire. Waiting in the gate area when I arrived with the captain and second officer after our layover in the President Hotel in Boston, unexpectedly, my brother, Dave, his wife, Mary, their sons, Bryan and Todd, my mother and father, and the new bride and groom, were all waiting to board the same airplane I would be flying to Denver.

When I checked in for my trip the previous day, I had no idea that it was a Boston layover or that the captain would ask me to fly the first leg to Chicago. The captain flew to Boston, so after the layover, it was my leg to Denver. Two things that had never happened in my career with Continental Airlines: One, crew scheduling called me the night before my scheduled trip and asked me to take a different trip. Two, as a first officer, no captain had ever asked me to fly the first leg of a trip.

This unlikely gathering of my eight family members were all traveling on special, fifty-dollar, one-way, non-refundable, space-available passes, which could only be purchased by Continental employees. It was an obvious scam, concocted by Continental's CEO, Frank Lorenzo, to bilk cash from CAL employees before filing his inevitable chapter-eleven bankruptcy, which would render any unused passes worthless.

On September 1, 1983, I took a chance on the passes. The passes only needed to be valid until September 24, another 23 days. This would give everyone valid passes for a week after the wedding, giving them time to travel around New England for a few days after the wedding. Dee and I had to go back to Denver right after the wedding because I had a trip scheduled in a few days.

Even though the passes were still valid on the 24th, the probability that any of my family members would get on my flight suddenly vanished to zip! The flight was oversold, meaning even some passengers with full-fare tickets would get bumped.

I went up to the podium and explained the situation to the gate agent. I asked if there was any chance that my family might be able to get out of Boston that day. I knew there was no way they would get on my flight. The gate agent looked at his computer screen and shook his head. He said, "I'll see what I can do."

I went out to the cockpit and we finished our preflight checks. When the gate agent was ready to button up the aircraft, he stuck his head in the cockpit and gave me a thumbs-up! "Got 'em all on." He said. The rumors were running wild, and we all knew the end was near.

The gate agent must have decided, *Screw it! I might as well do what I can to take care of other employees.* I know it wouldn't have happened, though, if crew scheduling hadn't asked me to change my scheduled trip, and I was able to tell the gate agent that all of these standby passengers were my relatives.

The captain was handling the radio communications with air traffic control (ATC), and I was flying the airplane and making all the public address

(PA) announcements. It was like a private chartered Boeing 727 for my family members.

We were vectored over a tip of Canada, north of the Great Lakes—my mother was born in Canada. When we were over Chicago, the ATC controller changed our route, clearing us on an airway that I hadn't been on in years—it goes over my hometown, Waterloo, Iowa. It was a beautiful, clear fall day. I made a PA over two of our family's favorite places, Strawberry Point and Devil's Backbone State Park.

After passing over Waterloo, a solid cloud layer formed beneath us. We never saw the ground again until landing in Denver. When the captain checked in with Denver Center, the controller asked, "Hey, Continental, what are you doing way north of your route?" We all three looked at each other. We all had heard the clearance from the Chicago controller. The captain keyed his mic, "We were cleared on this airway by Chicago Center."

"Okay, I don't have it on my strip." The Denver controller then gave us a vector to get back on our normal route. Shortly after checking in with

Denver Center, the solid undercast was joined by a solid overcast above us.

We were sandwiched in a thin layer of clear air, between two thick cloud layers. In front of the aircraft was a large cumulus cloud in the distance. The Sun was shining on the cloud, giving it a bright gold rim. In both directions, left and right, the bright gold transitioned into orange-yellow, then dark red, then deep purple. Abeam the aircraft on both sides, it was dark as night, even though it was mid-day. It was the most beautiful visual display I have ever seen in all of my flying experiences.

We were cleared for a straight-in ILS (instrument landing system) approach to runway 27-Right at Stapleton Airport. I clicked off the autopilot and punched through the top surface of the cloud deck. The air was smooth, the airplane was trimmed, and I was flying with slight, almost imperceptible, adjustments on the controls.

I had it wired! On glide-slope, on-course, on-speed. We broke through the cloud ceiling at 200 feet above the ground. Runway centerline was straight ahead. A perfect approach. At fifty feet above the runway, all hell broke loose. The airplane started rolling one direction—and then the other. We must have hit wake turbulence from another airplane. I was fighting to keep from hitting a wingtip on the runway.

Then, I heard the anti-skid circuit breakers clicking in the overhead panel above the captain's head. This was my only clue that the airplane was on the runway and the wheels were spooling up. I pulled up on the forward knobs on the three thrust levers, putting all three engines in idle reverse thrust.

It was the best landing I had ever made in any airplane. It was also my last landing as an airline pilot. My family got off in Denver. The captain flew to San Jose, where we had a layover. Dee called me later that night at the hotel. She told me Lorenzo shut the airline down. I no longer had a job. No, I didn't lose a job, I lost my identity—my self-esteem—my self-worth. That's another story—my total meltdown, the slow rehabilitation—for another time, maybe.

To bring perspective to this episode, I've made a rough estimate of the probability of that last flight happening as it did. The probability of any one event happening in a particular way can be expressed as a fraction, with the top number (numerator) equal to one, and the bottom number (denominator) being the total estimated number of events you would expect to have before the event would happen the way it did.

For a conjunction of unusual events, the overall probability of all events having their unusual outcome is found by multiplying all individual probabilities together.

For the flight described above, the following probabilities were estimated:

Crew Scheduling asked me to change my regular scheduled trip—it had never happened before, but I gave it a one chance out of ten (1/10).

Unexpected Boston layover, another ten percent. The accumulated probability for both of these first conditions occurring together is $1/10^2$.

I was the flying pilot on the flight from Boston to Denver. This only happened because the captain asked me to start out the trip by flying to Chicago. While this had never happened in over ten years as a copilot with Continental, I'll give it another ten percent chance, making the probability of the conjunction of these three circumstances $1/10^3$.

Even though none of the eight family members on this flight had ever been on one of my flights, I gave each family member a ten percent chance, so collectively, having all eight on the same flight had a probability of $1/10^8$.

The chance of a space-available pass rider getting on an oversold flight is slim to nil. To be conservative, I gave each family member a ten percent chance, so the chance of all eight getting on with SA passes is another $1/10^8$.

Multiplying the above three probabilities of mutual occurrences, the combined probability is one over ten to the nineteenth power—a '1' followed by nineteen zeros.

This probability (one, in ten to the nineteenth) was the probability of the requisite conjunction of events that occurred before we even released the brakes! For the coincidences during the flight, I assigned the following probabilities to each in-flight event:

Flying over Canada, where my mother was born $1/10^2$.

Chicago Center routed us over Waterloo, IA $1/10^2$.

ATC controller did not pass the clearance on to the next sector $1/10^2$.

The most phenomenal visual display of any flight in my career $1/10^2$.

Best-ever landing occurring just after flying through turbulence $1/10^2$.

The above five in-flight one-percent probabilities multiply the denominator by ten to the tenth power, bringing the overall probability $1/10^{29}$.

The mass of a gold atom is approximately $3.3/10^{25}$ kg/gold atom. The mass of 'ten-to-the twenty-ninth' gold atoms is, therefore, $3.3/10^{25} \times 10^{29} = 33{,}000$ kg.

The probability of all the above circumstances occurring on any single flight in my Continental Airline career is less than one chance in ten to the twenty-ninth power. This is equivalent to picking one individual gold atom out of 33,000 kilograms of gold.

The above calculation does not include the improbability of the flight being my last flight as an airline pilot.

My take away? The conjunction of highly improbable events seems to violate the second law of thermodynamics. Entropy, the measure of disorder in a system, should always increase. Extremely improbable events are like watching an ice cube spontaneously form in a glass of water on a hot day. It isn't prohibited by the laws of physics, but it is unimaginably improbable. I think it boils down to a question of stability.

Consider two experiments using a marble:

In the first, place a marble on the edge of a concave, hemispherical bowl. The marble rolls down to the bottom of the bowl, continuing up the other side, oscillating with decreasing amplitude until coming to rest at the bottom of the bowl. Once at rest, the initial condition can not be determined by an independent observer.

In the second, turn the hemispherical bowl upside-down, and place the marble at the top. The slightest disturbance will cause the marble to roll in some random direction, stopping at some distance away from the bowl. After this experiment, an independent observer could determine that the marble started at the top of the bowl (the initial condition) from its distance from the bowl.

In the first case, we can predict the future. In the second case, we can only predict the past. Built into the physics of any stable process seems to include a temporal reversal of cause and effect. (The future stable state appears to *cause* the various *effects* of many past events.)

11

Trouble with Harry

Almost every exciting flight with Continental Airlines, I was flying as copilot with Harry. When I would get back from a flight with Harry, Dee wouldn't ask, "How was your flight?" she'd always ask, "What happened this time?"

We'd had an epileptic seizure, a hijacking threat, engine fire warning, an elevator stuck on one side so the airplane rolled during rotation on takeoff—you name it. Maybe it was just when he was flying with me, but every fifteen minutes, Harry would do a full cockpit scan. One time, Harry reached over the center console to press the two "Press to test" hydraulic warning lights on the panel in front of me. They both lit up when he pressed them, but then one stayed on when he released them.

I drew an imaginary line forward on the centerline of the overhead panel, down the centerline of the forward instrument panel, and aft along the centerline of the pedestal. "Damn it, Harry, if you want me to check anything on this side of this line, just tell me and I'll do it, but don't touch anything on my side of the cockpit!"

One flight, we were inbound to LAX at 24,000 ft over the Grand Canyon. A contrail appeared just above the horizon at twelve o-clock, dead ahead. At first, the contrail looked like it was climbing, then it started descending toward the horizon and split into four contrails! Both of us realized at the same time that it was a formation of four fighters, at our altitude, and they had us bore-sighted.

Harry and I looked at each other with our palms up—sign language for, "What the hell do we do now?" The fighters were more maneuverable than our Boeing, and any change in course or altitude we made might have been in the same direction the fighters might choose. Our only hope was that the lead pilot would make the right decision in time.

The lead pilot figured it out just in time. He split the formation—two broke left, two broke right. They were four marine Phantom F4s, so close we could have read their names stenciled beneath their canopy rails, if we had time.

I reported the near-miss to ATC. The controller asked how close they were. Harry said, "About three hundred feet." The second officer said, "Yea, about a hundred yards." I keyed my mic and said, "Somewhere between three-hundred feet and a hundred-yards."

After a pause, the controller said, "Well, that's calling it pretty close."

A few years later, Dee and I were at a party, and I told this story. One of the women said, "The lead in that formation was my ex-husband! If you think it was scary for you, you should hear how big a 707 looks closing head-on, at over twelve-hundred knots!"

12

Dee's Nightmare

Sometime in 2009, the first year of Obama's presidency, Dee was teaching at Bal Swan school in Broomfield, and I was teaching at the United Training Center in Denver on the Boeing 747-400. From our home on the West side of Broomfield, Dee had to cross highway US 287 on Miramonte Blvd.

Dee was having a recurring nightmare about a big-rig truck running a red light, coming at her from a blind spot on her right side. She had told me about the dream several times, and she was getting really spooked at that intersection.

One weekday, I had the day off and picked Dee up to take her to lunch at KFC. From Bal Swan school, we were heading west on US 287 and needed to make a left turn at Greenway Dr. As I pulled into the left turn lane, a semi-truck was stopped in the opposite left turn lane, waiting for his green left arrow.

I got my left turn arrow first. I pulled in front of the stopped semi and was about to cross the eastbound lanes of US 287 when Dee said, "What about the other car?" I stopped immediately and asked, "What other—" Before I could finish, another big rig came out of nowhere! He had to be doing 70, trying to beat the red light. He couldn't have missed the front of our Prius by more than a foot.

After that, Dee never had that dream again.

13

On Thin Ice

One winter day when I was sixteen or seventeen (1955 or 1956), after a couple months of subzero temperature, I decided it would be fun to drive my metallic green '37 Chevy coupe on the Cedar River. I found a boat ramp that was not being used and drove down the boat ramp out onto the ice. I was right—it was great fun—getting up to speed—cramping the steering wheel, and tapping the brake.

I'd practice putting my car into spins and then recovering by matching the direction of the front wheels with the direction the wheels were sliding. Little did I know that this experience would someday help save a Boeing 727, with a full load of passengers.

We were approaching Peoria airport at night. Breaking action was reported 'fair' by a pilot of a small twin turboprop. The report was two hours old, and besides, those airplanes can stop on a dime without using brakes. Anyway, that was the only information we had. Peoria Approach didn't mention they had had freezing rain and that there was a half inch of ice coating everything.

On final, the runway lights were brighter than usual. They were shining through crystal clear glaze ice. There was a slight crosswind from the left. After touchdown, and going into reverse thrust, the airplane weather-cocked into the wind. Reverse thrust was backing us off the centerline toward the right side of the runway.

To drive back to the centerline, I took all three engines out of reverse, into idle forward thrust. Back on the centerline, the airplane had continued to weathercock, now almost perpendicular to the runway. *This is good—I'm on the centerline—I'll just keep it turning left.* I put #1 back into idle reverse. *With #2 and #3 in idle forward thrust, I'll still have a net forward thrust to cancel the left crosswind, and a net counter-clockwise torque from differential thrust to keep the airplane turning left.*

As the aircraft heading approached the reciprocal of the approach course, I put #1 back into idle forward thrust to slow the turn rate. Still on centerline, but now pointed back toward the touchdown zone, I pushed all three thrust levers forward to full forward thrust and stopped the airplane while it was sliding backward. It all happened in slow motion.

14

Future Causality

All these stories in *Insubordinate* are connected by a common thread—they all demonstrate that our perception that future events are caused by events in the past is an illusion of our consciousness. Each story describes an improbable future event that was only made possible by some subconscious foreshadowing or precognition. Information must have been transmitted from the future into the past.

A 1962 check ride that could not have been passed but for someone deciding to give an old beat-up Link trainer to East Waterloo High School in 1956. Somehow, information from the check ride must have been received by the exact right person at the right time.

My decision to abandon my plan to fly the hottest jet I could get my hands on, with the hope of getting into test pilot school at PAX River, and maybe even having a chance of being an astronaut. What did Mike know about the future that I didn't?

I don't expect you to buy my story about Bob, the invisible time-traveling monkey, but *something* compelled me to insist that Dee get a babysitter and go to that VP-48 squadron party. Without that, I never would have known that our MAYDAY had been received—and ignored.

It goes on and on! Was Dee's recurring dream a future memory of a truck that had not yet run the red light on US 287? Did the wife of the lead pilot of the formation of Phantom jets have a recurring dream of that future party and remembered my story that I had not yet told of the near miss that had not yet occurred? Did she tell her husband? Did that make him hyperattentive, and better prepared?

Incredulous as it might seem, based on our perception of time, we must admit that an ability to receive information from the future would be a valuable survival skill. Our genetic neural network is designed to learn from the collective experiences of our ancestors.

I would argue that the primary goal of the vast majority of DNA code is dedicated to solving the question, "What's going to happen next?"

No law of physics prohibits information from being transmitted in reverse time, in fact, it is a fundamental concept of quantum physics. The photon is now accepted as being its own antiparticle, and the only differentiating characteristic of an antiparticle, is that it appears to be propagated in reverse time.

Any physical mechanism that is allowed by physics will be co-opted by the genetic algorithm to hone survival skills. It is likely that we all have this skill to varying degrees, whether we are aware of it or not.

Lord Nelson is remembered for his quote, "I owe all my success in life to arriving a quarter-hour ahead of time." That's why the Navy starts all four-hour duty watches fifteen minutes early. Did Lord Nelson have the ability to see fifteen minutes into the future?

I have observed that women are more tuned in to information from the future than men. I'm no geneticist, but I think it is because women have two X chromosomes, while men have an X and a Y. The Y chromosome is nonrecombinant and does not evolve. A man's Y chromosome is identical to his father's, his father's, and his father's, all the way back on the paternal edge of a man's family tree.

A woman's egg has one X chromosome, which is a recombination of her two XX chromosomes. A daughter results when the egg is fertilized by a man's X sperm. The man's X chromosome came from his mother (the daughter's paternal grandmother), which was a recombination of her mother's two X chromosomes one generation before.

This recombination, or code swapping, is one way that our human genome learns from our ancestors and hones its strategy for survival.

Women evolve faster than men not only because they have two X, code-swapping genes, where men only have one, but traditionally, the generational cycle time is faster for women than for men. For example, if the average age of all your mothers and grandmothers were twenty when they gave birth to your ancestors, you would have one hundred mothers and grandmothers on your matriarchal line of ancestry in the last two thousand years. If the average age of all the fathers and grandfathers were thirty when your ancestors were born, it would have taken three thousand years to get one hundred fathers and grandfathers on your patriarchal line of ancestry.

Information, or thoughts, transmitted backward through time is a form of time travel. I propose that this form of time travel is not only possible but is *necessary* to prevent the grandfather paradox. Information from the future must get back to the past to make sure the past happens the way it had to happen, to allow the future to create itself.

Every event seems to be entangled with every other event, future and past. This infinite network of entangled events makes the past as much dependent on the future as visa-versa.

I have always felt that Dee is more evolved than I am. She is certainly more intuitive, and has probably saved my life more times than I realize.

15

First Pre-flight of a Boeing 707

My first line trip as a nugget second officer (flight engineer) was a night departure from Gate 68 in LAX. All of my training sessions had been in daylight, so this was the first time I had been up close and personal with a 707 at night.

I had turned over a new leaf, hoping for more success with my new Continental Airline career, than what I had in the Navy. I had a brand new uniform, a new London Fog (with a warm, zip-in liner), and a new triple-D, black anodized Maglite. I even had shiny black shoes. I was squared away!

In the cockpit, I stowed my new leather flight bag (Brain-Bag), and hung the London Fog. (Overkill for LAX, but we were headed to ORD, and it was January.) I probably would have left the London Fog in the cockpit even if it was freezing. It was my first chance to show off my new Continental flight-officer uniform, which to most civilians, looked like a full USN Commander's uniform.

I know, it sounds vindictive. Petty resentment of a system that measures a person's competence by the amount of gold braid on their sleeves. But, I was young and still raw from the insult of being passed over for lieutenant. My resentment had not yet matured into full-blown cynicism.

I descended the stairs at the end of the passenger boarding walkway (jetway). The captain and first officer were in the Flight Operations office. We always started our walk-around preflight inspection at the left main landing gear.

When I shined my flashlight on the first tire I encountered, I was shocked! The first three layers of cords were showing through the tread. I moved the beam of my Maglite to the other three tires—they were all the same. They were the rattiest set of tires I'd ever seen—worse than the tires on my '37 Chevy!

Then I tried to find the other things I was supposed to check. The shiny steel cylindrical surface of the oleo strut wasn't even visible! I couldn't see anything I recognized. No tire pressure gauge, no brake-puck wear pins. Everything was coated with thick grease. I thought, *This is a bait-and-switch. Welcome to the real world.*

Then, the deal breaker! The entire landing gear assembly was twisted! It was almost perpendicular to the direction of the airplane. I was just about to go into Flight Ops to tell the captain that this aircraft was not going anywhere with me on it!

Luckily, before I stormed into Ops, the beam of my Maglite swept across the sidewall of one of the tires. Stenciled around the side of the tire was, "JETWAY—JETWAY—JETWAY." I looked up at the huge glass windows in the passenger boarding area. There were about a hundred passengers watching me walking around the jetway tires, with obvious concern.

I was embarrassed, at first, but by the time I finished my exterior preflight, I had rationalized it and figured they probably felt pretty good about getting on the aircraft. *By the time that kid gets to the real airplane, nothing is going to get by him, if he's that careful about the jetway.*

I always wanted a cool nickname like, "Maverick," or "IceMan," or "Goose," but "Jetway" was never on my short list. I've often thought about how the course of my life would have changed if I had dragged the captain out of Ops to show him the jetway tires. I vowed to not repeat that same mistake—I never shined my shoes again.

I have been saved by an infinite number of small (sometimes stupid) decisions, without which I would have been led on widely divergent futures. All of those small decisions had to occur in their proper order, at their proper time, to trace the unique space time path I have traveled. I am convinced that without guidance, I would not have survived.

Years ago, Dee received a fortune cookie that said, "Experience increases wisdom but does not reduce folly." We used that fortune for a label on a V-file in our file cabinet. Over the years, the file continued to grow from reminders of dumb mistakes (mostly mine), like buying Holly Corp. stock on a tip from a pilot. The company bought the London Bridge, to reconstruct it across the Colorado River near Lake Havasu. I thought it was going to be the historic "Tower Bridge." Wrong bridge—the stock tanked.

Human intelligence will always have an advantage over artificial intelligence. We learn more from mistakes than we learn from success. A.I. must rely more on success for training its neural network, since it is easier to measure. The infinite consequences of human error cannot be anticipated by a machine.

I have come to believe that every event is entangled with every other event, both future and past. The future can only be created by the exact sequence of past events, and that exact sequence of past events could only have happened with guidance from the future.

16

Machu Picchu

The first long vacation Dee and I took was about a year and a half after starting to fly for Continental Airlines. In early September, 1968, we got inter-line passes on a Peruvian Airline. Our plan was to first go to Lima and then a side trip to Cusco and Machu Picchu. Our plan after Machu Picchu was to go back to Lima and fly across the Andes to Rio de Janeiro, for a total of two weeks in South America.

When we got to the hotel in Lima, it was so horrible, we checked the flight schedule, got a taxi, went back to the airport, and got on a flight to Rio. When we got to the hotel in Rio (very nice—right on Ipanema Beach), we had been awake for about twenty-nine hours. It was late morning, and we were wide awake, but tired.

Dee and I donned our swimming suits and grabbed a couple of towels. Ipanema was vacant at its closest shore to our hotel—the crowd was about a quarter mile down the beach to our right. Dee sat on the beach and watched me walk out to waist-high water. I didn't intend to swim much, just a few strokes.

Suddenly, I couldn't touch the bottom. Dee was getting smaller. I realized that I was in a rip tide, going out toward Sugar Loaf faster than I could swim. I waved at Dee. She waved back. I turned left, to parallel the beach, and started swimming at a pace that I could maintain, while letting the rip tide carry me out further.

Fortunately, we had a pool at our house in San Diego, and my swimming endurance was greater than at any other time in my life. Eventually, I reached the area where most of the other swimmers were, and I was able to slowly work my way in to the shore.

Even if we had brought our Spanish dictionary to the beach, we wouldn't have been able to read the warning signs at Ipanema Beach. We were unaware that they were in Portuguese.

The point of narrating this episode is not about my survival of a dangerous rip tide at Ipanema so much as the accidental and fortunate delay of our visit to Machu Picchu by about a week.

Dee and I were standing in the main courtyard of Machu Picchu, viewing the Intihuatana Stone, *the hitching post of the sun.* A stone peg protruded out from one of the plane surfaces on the monolithic monument, and the shadow of the peg cast a shadow in the shape of an arrow. The point of the arrow fell dead on a deep groove across the flat stone surface.

I looked at my watch. It was twelve, noon. I asked Dee what day it was. "Twenty-first of September," she said. My knees almost buckled as I realized that we were (by pure accident) standing at the precise place, and precise time of the year, that the entire Machu Picchu complex was designed to measure.

Carved by the Incas, over five-hundred years earlier, the Intihuatana Stone was now marking the spring equinox for the southern hemisphere. It gave the Inca priests the knowledge to announce the proper time to plant crops—the source of their absolute power over their people.

This was secret knowledge, otherwise, Machu Picchu would not have been so inaccessible to the common Inca, and every farmer would have had a vertical stick stuck in the ground, with a small stone placed to its south, marking the equinox when the tip of the stick's shadow falls on the stone at midday.

Secret knowledge is always closely guarded by those who seek absolute power. Ironically, blackmail, mystic cult idolatry, or superstition eventually backfires. Fear and superstition always boomerang back on the keepers of secret knowledge. They live in constant fear that others might extrapolate their knowledge beyond their own capacity.

Those in power eventually fear their own secrets. They project what they would do with knowledge they do not understand.

Greater than a dictator's fear of their own ignorance, however, is their fear of women. Eventually, this fear will drive desperate attempts to concentrate male dominance in the centers of political, financial, and legal power in society.

But it will be too late.

Women will be their ultimate insubordinates.

Appendix

Circular Geometry from the Atom to Planetary Orbits

Synopsis

This appendix presents a geometric sequence linking several familiar quantities in atomic and orbital mechanics. Beginning with simple circular geometry, a numerical relation close to the fine-structure constant appears. The same constant determines the velocity of the electron in the Bohr model of hydrogen. Using Kepler's third law, a similar scaling appears in planetary motion, leading to a characteristic orbital velocity that can be compared with atomic constants.

1. Geometry of a Regular Polygon

For a regular polygon with N sides, the central angle subtended by one side is $\theta = \dfrac{2\pi}{N}$.

If N=861 then $\theta = \dfrac{2\pi}{861}$.

Numerically, $\dfrac{2\pi}{861} \approx 0.007298$.

The fine-structure constant is $\alpha \approx \dfrac{1}{137} \approx 0.007299$.

Thus $\alpha \approx \dfrac{2\pi}{861}$.

For a polygon with unit sides, the radius of the circumscribed circle is $R = \dfrac{1}{2\sin(\pi/N)}$.

With $\mathrm{N} = 861, R \approx 137$.

Thus a polygon with **861 unit sides produces a circle whose radius is very close to 137 units**, linking the geometry of the circle with the numerical value of the fine-structure constant.

2. Circular Motion in the Bohr Model

In the Bohr model of hydrogen, the electron in the ground state moves in a circular orbit with velocity $v = \alpha c$.

Thus the fine-structure constant determines the ratio between the electron's orbital velocity and the speed of light.

The Bohr quantization condition is: $m_e v a_0 = \hbar$.

If the circulation of the orbit is defined as $\Gamma = v(2\pi a_0)$, then

multiplying by the electron mass gives: $m_e \Gamma = m_e v(2\pi a_0)$.

Substituting the Bohr condition gives: $\hbar = m_e \dfrac{\Gamma}{2\pi}$.

This allows Planck's constant to be interpreted as **mass multiplied by circulation** for the electron orbit.

3. Circular Motion in Planetary Orbits

Planetary motion around the Sun follows Kepler's third law:

$$T^2 = \frac{4\pi^2}{GM} R^3 .$$

Orbital velocity is: $$V = \frac{2\pi R}{T} .$$

Analysis of several approximately two-body solar orbits suggests an approximate integer sequence for orbital radii:

$$R_N = N^2 R_{\min} .$$

Substituting into Kepler's law gives: $T_N = N^3 T_{\min}$.

Using the velocity equation then gives:

$$V_N = \frac{V_\Gamma}{N} \text{ where } V_\Gamma = \frac{2\pi R_{\min}}{T_{\min}} .$$

Gravitational acceleration becomes: $g_N = \dfrac{g_{\max}}{N^4}$.

Thus four simple scaling relations appear:

$$V_N = \frac{V_\Gamma}{N}$$

$$R_N = R_{\min} N^2$$

$$T_N = T_{\min} N^3$$

$$g_N = \frac{g_{\max}}{N^4} .$$

4. Empirical Velocity Scale

Using orbital data for several solar system bodies that most closely approximate two-body motion gives $V_\Gamma \approx 144$ km/s. Bodies used in the estimate include:

Body	Approximate N
Mercury	3
Mars	6
Ceres	8
Jupiter	11
Saturn	15

Venus and Earth were excluded because they form a strongly coupled pair exhibiting an approximate **8-year resonance**.

5. Comparison with Atomic Constants

Dividing the velocity scale by the speed of light gives:

$$\frac{V_\Gamma}{c} \approx 4.8 \times 10^{-4}.$$

The square of three times the fine-structure constant is:

$$(3\alpha)^2 \approx 4.79 \times 10^{-4}.$$

Thus $V_\Gamma \approx (3\alpha)^2 c$ to within the scatter of the planetary data.

Whether this numerical agreement reflects a deeper physical connection or a coincidence is left as an open question.

6. Final Observation

One notable feature of Kepler's law is that bodies of very different mass follow the same orbital scaling. For example, both the dwarf planet **Ceres** and the giant planet **Jupiter** follow the same Kepler scaling in their motion around the Sun. This is analogous to Galileo's observation that the period of a pendulum depends on its length and the gravitational acceleration, but not on the mass of the pendulum bob.

These examples suggest that the trajectories themselves are properties of the surrounding gravitational-inertial geometry. In this sense, the path followed by an orbiting body is determined primarily by the structure of the field rather than by the mass of the orbiting object.

Charles deAnne

www.ingramcontent.com/pod-product-compliance
Lightning Source LLC
LaVergne TN
LVHW020636100826
845148LV00012B/2198

* 9 7 9 8 2 1 8 4 5 2 2 5 4 *